HAPPY HANUKAH!

To: _____

From: _____

Date: _____

Grateful acknowledgment is made to BMG Chrysalis Company for permission to reprint "Honeyky Hanukah" by Woody Guthrie.
Text © 2003 Woody Guthrie Publications, Inc. (BMI). All Rights Administered by BUG Music, Inc.,
a BMG Chrysalis company. Used by Permission. All Rights Reserved.

Visit us on the Web! randomhouse.com/kids

Educators and librarians, for a variety of teaching tools, visit us at RHTeachersLibrarians.com

Library of Congress Cataloging-in-Publication Data
Guthrie, Woody.
Honeyky Hanukah / Woody Guthrie, Dave Horowitz. — First edition.
pages   cm.
Summary: A family celebrates Hanukkah with latkes, hugs, kisses, and dancing.
ISBN 978-0-385-37926-7 (trade) — ISBN 978-0-375-97339-0 (lib. bdg.) — ISBN 978-0-375-98239-2 (ebook)
1. Children's songs, English—United States—Texts. [1. Hanukkah—Songs and music. 2. Songs.] I. Horowitz, Dave, illustrator. II. Title.
PZ8.3.G9635Ho 2014   782.42083—dc23 [E] 2013045762

The illustrations for this book were created with construction paper, charcoal, and colored pencils.
Book design by Nicole de las Heras

MANUFACTURED IN CHINA
10 9 8 7 6 5 4 3 2 1
First Edition

WOODY GUTHRIE
HONEYKY HANUKAH

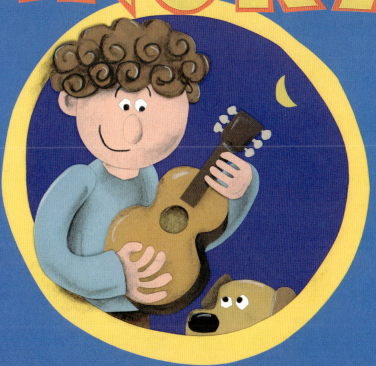

pictures by Dave Horowitz

Doubleday Books for Young Readers

It's Honeyky Hanukah 'round and around,
Honeycake Hanukah, eat them down,

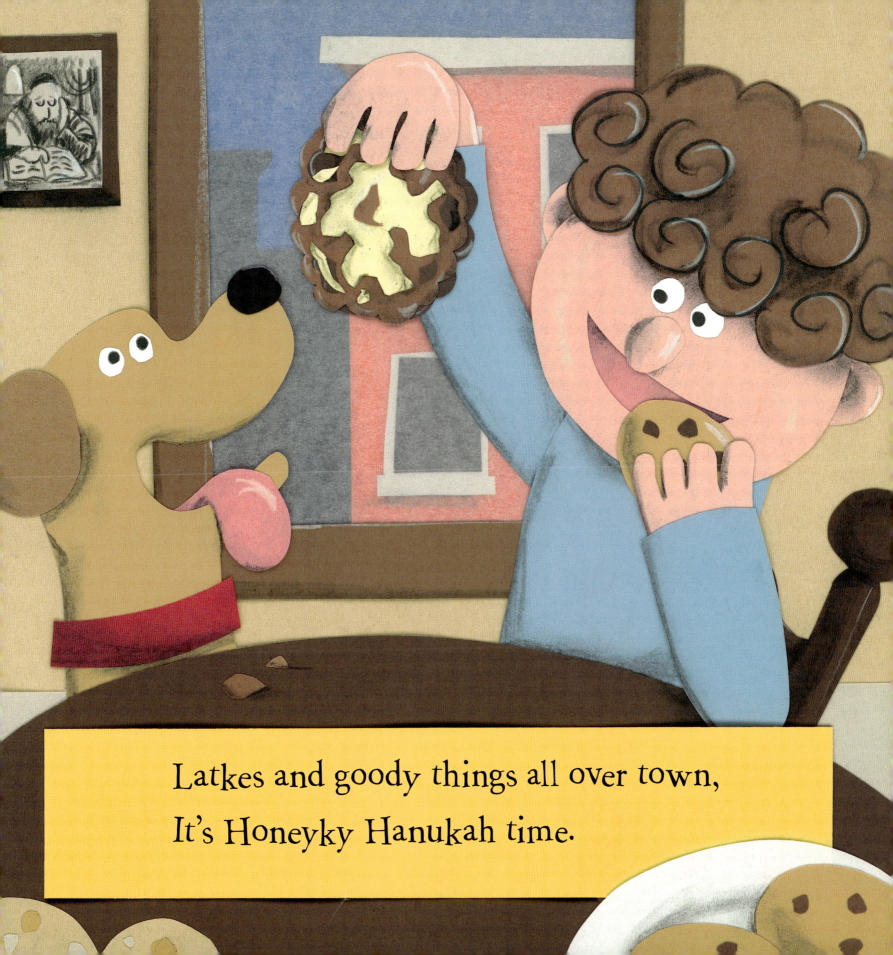

Latkes and goody things all over town,
It's Honeyky Hanukah time.

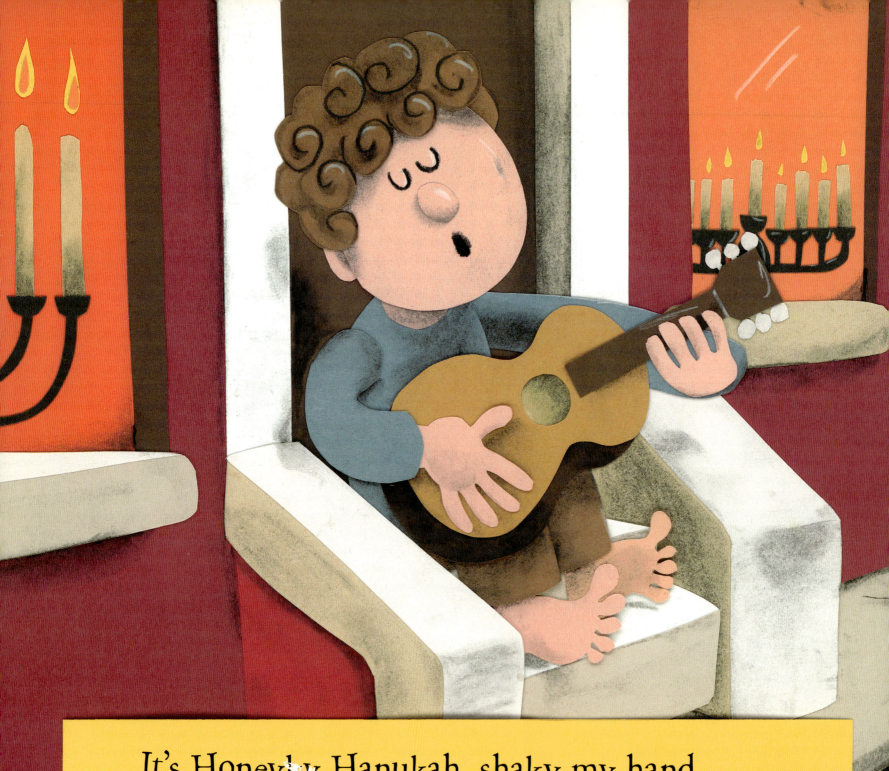

It's Honeyky Hanukah, shaky my hand,
My candles are burning all over this land,

To light the dark road for the man passing by,
It's Honeyky Hanukah time.

It's Honeyky Hanukah, kissy my cheek,
The light in my window, it burns for a week,

I'll open my present and take a little peek,
It's Honeyky Hanukah time.

It's Honeyky Hanukah, makes me feel glad,
This box for Mother and this box for Dad,

For sister and brother, nice ribbons I'll tie,
It's Honeyky Hanukah time.

It's Honeyky Hanukah, huggy me tight,
It's Hanukah day, and it's Hanukah night,

It's Honeyky Hanukah, kiss me some more,
We'll sing and go dancing around on the floor,

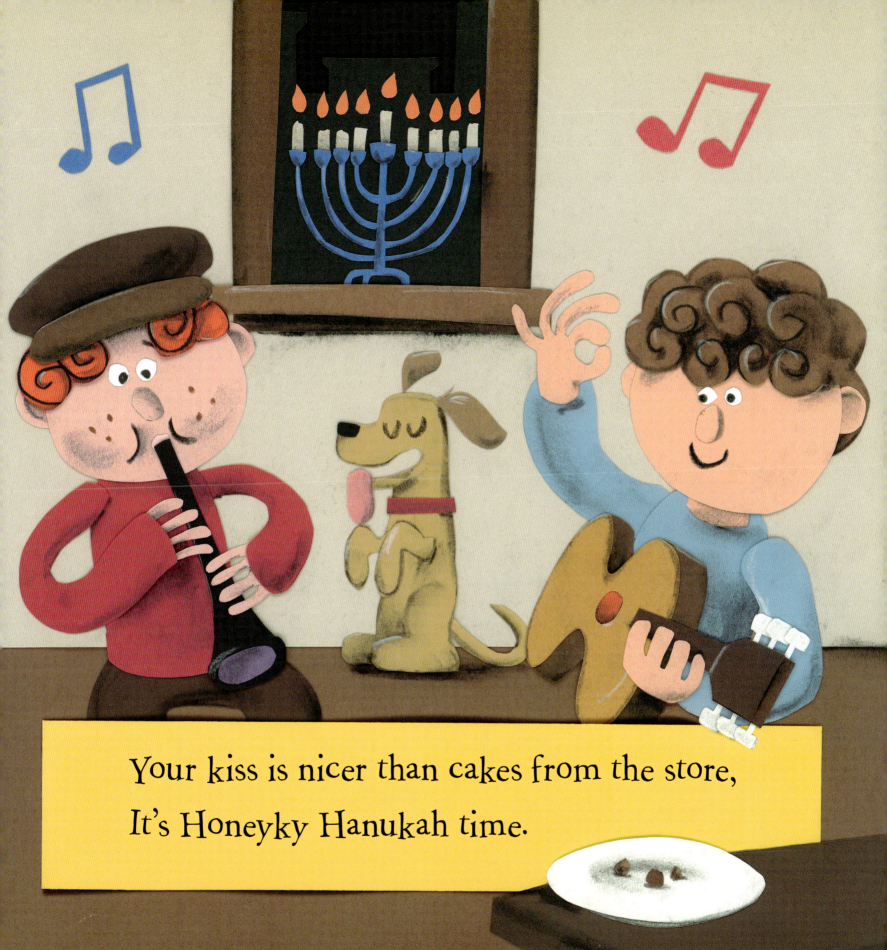

Your kiss is nicer than cakes from the store,
It's Honeyky Hanukah time.

It's Honeyky Hanukah, brushy my hair,
Let's dance a big hora and jump in the air,

You look lots prettier to me every year
At Honeyky Hanukah time.

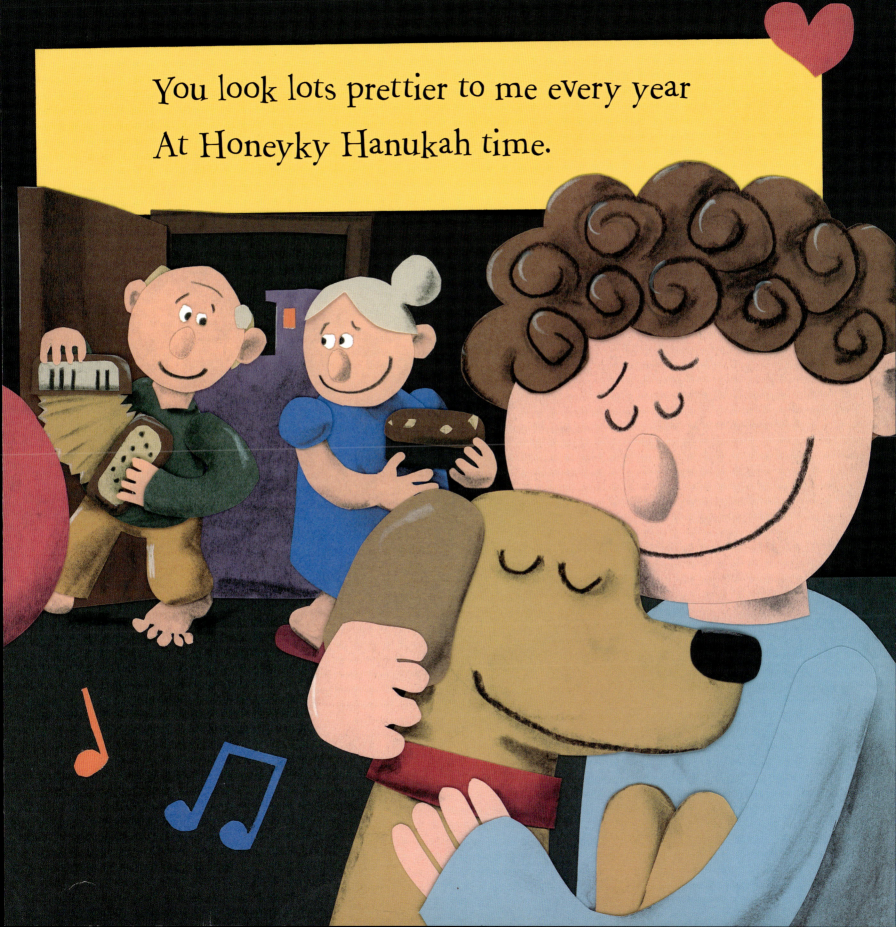

A Coney Island Hanukah: Woody Guthrie's New York Story

Woody Guthrie's Jewish songs can be traced to his friendship with his mother-in-law, Aliza Greenblatt, a well-known Yiddish poet who lived down the street from Woody and his family in Coney Island, New York, in the 1940s. Woody and Aliza often discussed their artistic projects and critiqued each other's work, finding common ground in their shared love for culture and social justice. Here is the story of how their unlikely collaboration began.

In 1942, Sophie Maslow, a dancer who had performed with the Martha Graham Dance Company, choreographed a suite for the New Dance Group using some of Woody's songs. She and Marjorie Mazia, another dancer with the troupe, went to Woody's Greenwich Village apartment to invite him to perform at the premiere. According to Guthrie family legend, Marjorie and Woody fell in love during the rehearsals. They moved to Coney Island in June 1943 to be near Marjorie's parents, Aliza and Isadore Greenblatt.

Aliza played a major role in the Guthrie family's life. Known as Bubbie (the Yiddish word for *grandma*), Aliza cared for her grandchildren and held Friday-night Sabbath dinners. Woody saw a strong connection between the Jewish struggle and that of his fellow Oklahomans during the

Dust Bowl, and was inspired to write songs that celebrated Jewish culture. He performed his Hanukah songs at local Jewish community centers and wrote other songs about Jewish history, spiritual life, World War II, and the anti-fascist cause.

At the bottom of the handwritten lyrics for "Honeyky Hanukah," Woody signed:

Woody Guthrie
3520 Mermaid Avenue
Brooklyn, 24, New York
November 21, 1949

Woody Guthrie lived in Coney Island for seven years. The songs he wrote there—full of his love for family and home—convey to us today the stories of a bygone time.

Woody and Marjorie Mazia Guthrie, circa 1944

Courtesy of Nora Guthrie